REMOTE CONTROL

R. R. Angell

This book is a work of fiction. Any references to historical events, real people, or real places are used fictitiously. Names, characters, places, and events are products of the author's imagination, and any resemblance to actual events or places or persons or animals, living or dead, is purely coincidental.

ISBN-13: 978-1-949532-00-5

Cover design by Teagan Gavet

Published in the United States by Sisu Publications

www.sisupublications.com

This story originally appeared in Interzone Science Fiction and Fantasy magazine Issue 216

Reprinted by permission of the author.

Dedicated to every
dreamer.

REMOTE CONTROL

It happened right in the middle of my shift. I'd been flipping, as usual, through the thirty-two thumbnails of empty, peaceful desert arrayed across the bottom of my wall screen. The map of my surveillance territory encompassed 1,000 Atco-Johnson Perimeter Stations that ruled 62 miles of Mexican border; one station every 100 meters. Thirty-two stations were awake; the rest were waiting for proximity sensors to give them something to do.

The border alarms down near the town of Las Cruce went off and two perimeter alarms turned red on my screen, the ones around them turned yellow. That made a three hundred meter ingress, so it was either a lot of runners, a few runners spread far apart, or a herd of something.

So then the fun started. The big screen switched automatically to the closest Johnson, but I didn't see anything out there. Amber light washed over me from the alert board over my head, but nobody's asking questions yet.

"Yo, Mac. What's shaken over there?" my buddy, Dobson, said in the next workstation.

"Lemmings looking for a cliff, Dobie," I said.

"Coming my way?"

"Nope. All mine."

"Lucky stiff. I got no action for days."

"Here they come," I said, and like that the Johnson queues stacked right up, with most of them in a perfect distribution around the closest turret bot. How the riders know this shit, I'll never know. I couldn't see a thing.

It's all about the riders, mostly twelve to fifty-eight year-old guys, all angst and aggression with nowhere to put it. Women, between twenty-three and fifty-four, with clusters centered around thirty, forty, and fifty years of age, account for about twenty percent.

Used to be they surfed in on the web, but the controls were hard to work. Now they log in from home or from corporate playrooms on all the major gaming platforms, except for that one from a Buddhist company in Oregon. Patriots lined up by the millions in the stores, and then online.

I heard that some guy named Johnson came up with the Web-Cam-Servo-Rifle combo, but I don't know that for certain. Every Johnson bot is solar powered, and that really tears up the environmentalists; they don't know if they should applaud or protest. The Patriots got 'em outnumbered anyway, and with better slogans like "Protect Our Borders, Protect Our Jobs" they get all the good press. But they don't see what I see.

Who'd have thought folks would pay five bucks for three shots and the privilege of staring at empty desert landscapes for up to ten minutes? Most times they end up trimming the witch mesquite in their last thirty seconds. They've already killed just about every cactus within range.

The enviro people are all over us for that. Cactus huggers, my commander calls them, and the Saguaro Faction is especially nasty. At first, they wanted to go down there and put up shields to deflect the bullets. They lost three members in three attempts, and then realized it was hopeless. It's all in the hands of the lawyers now, and everyone has to certify they know they are using live ammunition at login.

The map down the left side of my screen showed the US border lit up with sensor lights. To the right was my field of Johnson turrets. The awake gunbots were bright green, the ones with riders blink.

The riders come in and queue up for the closest gun. When the queue hits three deep, it wakes up nearby guns so more riders can hop into a live gunbot.

It started with five riders, so I went to work and called up the stats by type and location.

Platform Code	Location
VR501	Calphalon, NJ
VR501	Billings, MT
612	Hainertown, MI
963	Dewey Beach, DE
UID	Unknown

At this time of day, the riders were most likely kids, but I ran the commerce checks anyway; standard ops, top to bottom.

The first rider was Robbie Tremo, 13, stepping in from a VR unit in Jersey. I knew him by the bragger profile he kept; no kills yet, but he scored a maiming on his last bullet on May seventeenth. Everyone in his junior high signed up after that.

The next kid was in a time zone where he should still be in school. I didn't boot him, but I wanted to. Not my job to judge the riders, just to monitor them, and the kid's credit was good. He might be out sick.

Next was Amy Saffel, 48 years old, in on a credit card through her husband's game station. She'd been on for over an hour doing her bit for Secure Our National Borders, or maybe she was blowing off steam. I guessed anger management over SONB since she was averaging less than five minutes for each three-round session. I had no idea what she was shooting at. Go get 'em, girl.

The fourth was just a guy in an internet café with a stolen credit card. The commerce checks on the first four come up with no surprises. It was that fifth one, the unidentified one, that triggered the alarms in my head.

So I contacted Legal, just like I'm supposed to do.

"Yeah, Station A47? What's the scoop?"

"I've got an unidentified Rider with no location," I said into my headset.

"I'll be right there." She clicked off. The situation light outside my station flashed orange.

The kid in Billings dropped his third round and was replaced by someone from Ontario, Canada. I terminated him immediately. Sometimes foreigners do get in, and maybe they squeeze off a round, but not on my watch. If one of them killed or maimed a runner, there would be all kinds of trouble. Like the training says, if someone breaks into your house and you kill them it is self-defense; a homeowner has the right to do that. They call it the Castle Precedent, and it changed the way we do everything.

Only Americans patrol our borders. It would be illegal otherwise.

Next thing I know, Legal is in the room. She's big, and old. Her lavender perfume surrounds me and I want to surrender and go get some fresh air.

"How many, Private?"

"The deepest queue right now is fifteen, Ma'am, but Johnsons are waking up all over the place and shifting the players." I pointed at the three staggered rows of gunbots. The little block of stats next to each one showed queue depth, time remaining, shots remaining in session, and barrel temperature.

Maintenance and reloading is automatic. Each bot can fire a round every ten seconds for a month without intervention or overheating. My sector was overdue and slated to be restocked next week, but activity this month had been low. Plenty of ammo left.

Legal pushed in next to me and poked at the border lights, the LCD wall dimpled under her finger.

"Please don't touch my screen, Ma'am," I said, pulling up the area distribution of riders. It made a perfect bell-curve around the ingress.

"Have you called Marketing?"

"No, Ma'am."

She popped her COM watch off her wrist and fiddled with it. I was still trying to see what had tripped the border sensors. I switched from gunbot view to a more powerful central camera and zoomed in as I elevated the lens. The image jerked back and forth.

"What's that? Wind? I don't see any wind out there."

"No, Ma'am. It's just my surveillance camera telescoping up. The riders saw something moving out there and shot at it. Some of them got lucky and hit me."

Marketing bounced into the room, a skinny, hyperactive guy named Mark. "Nice," he said. "We should put things out there for target practice. Bring in more happy riders."

Bring in more cash is what he meant. I heard they were raking in over ten million dollars a month with the rider software alone, not to mention a strong subscription base. That's a lot of surveillance. First time a government agency had ever run a profit.

Then there was the prison system. They set up rider-monitored kill zones around fifty terrorist prisons scattered across the country and successful escapes dropped to zero. Early in the program they had problems getting the guards in and out, but they fixed that. I can't say how, it's classified.

"What's going on here?" Mark the marketing guy said, tapping my screen where the distribution curve seemed to spike.

"I'm not sure, but don't touch my screen." I pulled up the stats on the Johnson with the oversized queue. It was the UID, and I decided to call him Rider One. The readout said Rider One had been in for thirteen minutes and taken five shots. "Looks like someone's getting a free ride. I'll boot him."

He didn't boot. I ran another commerce background check on him and came up with zilch. No name, no purchase profile, no credit history. Nothing. I called up his CPU registration mark. Nada.

"Who is this guy?" Legal said. "More importantly, where is he?"

I tried a different trace. Nothing. I couldn't tell if he was inside the country and that was bad.

"And why here?" Legal reached in and traced her finger over the map cutting a momentary trough of light through the riders.

"That's government property, Ma'am. Please, don't touch my screen." These people had no respect.

Then I saw the pattern.

"This guy, let's call him Rider One, isn't a guy at all."

"What do you mean?" Mark said.

"Look at the IP addresses for him. They are completely non-routable, and they shift like a kaleidoscope."

"And non-routable means?"

"An IP address like that has to be inside our own network to work, but it isn't. See here," I said, indicating the readouts. "Here's his signal. The trace says the packets are coming in from all over, not just by one or two routes. It's like confetti. That's why I can't boot him. Watch," I said.

I keyed the dump sequence and a second later Rider One disappeared.

"You were saying?" Legal said.

"Look!" Mark said, stabbing the screen two Johnsons up.

"Don't touch--"

"He's right there, at the head of the line!"

And damned if Mark wasn't right. Now, how the hell did Rider One do that? He disappeared and hopped to the front of the queue on another gunbot.

"There!"

Mark's hand jabbed for the screen and I caught it at the wrist. Mark whimpered. I have a strong grip. "Sorry, but what'd I say?"

Onscreen, Rider One jumped from Johnson to Johnson until it found the one closest to the ingress. In all the excitement, I'd almost forgotten that there were targets coming through the border perimeter. I zoomed in.

"I'll have to call the General," Ms. Legal heaved herself upright and fiddled with her COM watch.

A carpet of dirty sheep was surging across the desert border like the Kansas City Chiefs swarming over a virtual first-down line. The Johnsons were up and ready, locked and loaded, ready for action. And I could feel them all, like some sort of cyber-salivating multi-conscious force hell-bent on just one thing.

It was the perfect deterrent for runners. Except these were sheep, and they didn't have a clue until the first three feet of wool erupted in blood.

They panicked and scattered northwest, deeper into

the US kill-zone, blood-streaked sheep hopping over fallen bodies and getting blown apart in mid-air.

"The kids must love that," the Marketeer said, like he was in church. "Can you check to see how many slo-mo replays this is getting? That's the latest feature at a nickel a view, and it's accessible world-wide."

That got Legal's attention. "You're kidding, right?"

No answer, so I figure there must be a liability issue, but General Fanning stomped into the room right then. His chest medals clacked as he stopped behind me.

"At ease, Private," he ordered, not that I had time to salute or anything. "What are you doing, son?"

"I'm working up replay statistics for the marketing guy, Sir!" I put the results in a tiny window so Mark would have to squint, and slid it as far to the right as possible.

"Mutton for dinner, eh, Rose?" the General said, huffing a laugh behind me.

"I don't know, Randall. Do they make lamb enchiladas down there?"

The sheep were flying apart like some special effect in the latest New Zealand blockbuster.

"That's just plain wrong," the General said. "Did you guys install machine guns out there?"

The General was right, and not because of his rank this time. There were far too many bullets flying; Rider One was humping it out like there was no tomorrow, and his Johnson overheated and shut down. Then he disappeared, and some poor kid stepped in and had to wait for the barrel to cool. He could spend his whole ten minutes just looking around without being able to shoot.

The scene calmed, and the sheep steered further northwest behind a bloody wall of bodies. There was a slight breeze tickling the brush from the southwest, so the warning smell of carnage would be blowing away from the herd.

Marketing was happy. "Look at these replay numbers! I'll bet we're pulling in a grand-a-minute easy."

"Your assessment, Private?"

"Sir! It appears that there is an entity, Sir."

"Explain."

"My guess is that some kid-genius built a virtual machine in some university supercomputing cluster. Then he built an entity specifically for riding."

Legal leaned on my armrest. "Is this entity alive?" She was close enough to bite off my ear.

The scene on the screen was almost pastoral except for the desert and the bloody barricade. An occasional sheep would bloom red and fall down, so things were back to normal. No longer a barrage of bullets.

"This is great!" Marketing said. "This whole sector had silencers installed at last reload. They don't have a clue where the guns are."

I shot Mark an angry look. "Why'd you do that?"

"Better target maintenance," he said.

"As in keeping them in range longer?"

"Technically speaking, we make more that way; the queues are deeper. Not to mention that it's more effective."

"Shit," I said, shaking my head.

"Soldier! There is a lady present."

I begged to differ, but I'd take her over Marketing any day.

"Yes, Sir! Sorry, Ma'am."

She ignored me. "I asked you if this entity is alive."

"Not in the sense that it eats, pees, and--" I stopped myself. "No ma'am, not what you'd consider alive, though it can obviously interact with our reality."

"Could it be classified as a U.S. citizen?"

"No, Ma'am. I couldn't see anyone making that claim. It could be coming from anywhere in the world."

"Shit," she said. "Shit, shit, shit."

General Fanning kept quiet. I could hear his heavy breathing as we stared at the red pile of sheep. A hoof twitched hypnotically in the stack and I wanted to look away. The General ordered, "Show me the big picture, Soldier."

I zoomed out and the carnage wasn't so in-your-face, more like a rock wall, the kind you might see around a peaceful New England field.

That's when I noticed the boy, a stick figure at this magnification, stumbling toward the frontline, all limbs and angles and uncertain centers of gravity, off to help his sheep without a thought for himself.

The General grunted, Legal said, "Oh, no," and Marketing leaned closer. I kept my eye on him.

Then Rider One showed up on Johnson 329, the gun installation closest to the shepherd. I tried booting it with no luck, so I booted the riders from the three other guns within range of the boy.

"You can't do that," Marketing said. "That's illegal."

"Equipment malfunction. Let 'em prove otherwise," I said, glancing at Legal. She frowned, and I booted the next three riders while monitoring Rider One. It seemed to be tracking but not shooting, so I called up the view from its scope.

"The bastard is waiting for a better shot," I said. "Sorry, Ma'am. Do you think it knows I'm booting the others?"

"Private," said General Fanning. "Your job is to assess the riders, not to play God."

"We've got to stop him, Randy," Ms. Legal said. I nodded vigorously, as the kid jogged toward the gun at an oblique angle.

"Now, Rose--" The General sounded just like my dad had most nights.

"I mean it," she said. If this entity kills a human, it poses a liability we do not want to assume. It will be our fault. I can't think of a single legal maneuver that would stand up in court."

"It's trivial. The Private here will log all actions and then lead a team to prevent these encroachers from getting back in. Isn't that right, Private?"

"Sir! Yes, sir!" I made damned sure the log was logging.

"Randall," she said. "This little triviality could undermine the entire Presidential Directive. Mexico won't cooperate if it thinks in any way that forces outside the US are enforcing this border closure. They'll say it had to do with oil, like with the Canadians. How many companies have gone bankrupt without a labor force? Our economy can't hold out forever."

"Ms. Ehrenberg," General Fanning said, in a voice loud enough to stop conversations two cubicles over. "We are a resilient nation. Even with rampaging unemployment, we will survive."

"And we still can't find anyone to do the little jobs,"

she said. "What's wrong here, Randall?"

"We will do what we must do to maintain the integrity of these borders against illegal crossers and terrorists--"

"General Fanning," she interrupted, just like my mom. I was starting to like the old gal. "You and I both know that terrorists don't sneak across the desert. They come through looking like saints with the best papers money can buy, and then we scratch our heads wondering where we went wrong."

I kept on booting riders. The shepherd waded through the flock, Rider One tracking his every step.

"Escuse me, Sirs." Maria had come for the trash. "Escuse me." The General and Marketing shifted out of the way, and I saw Maria's hand reach in and grab the trashcan. I got a whiff of disinfectant, and then the can fell to the floor and I heard her gasp as she staggered back against the wall.

I didn't know anything about Maria's family, but I had an idea about where they were from. She was a good, hardworking woman.

Then a team of three riders stepped in from a corporate playroom. One took a shot, followed by the other two. All three missed, but a sheep went down next to the shepherd and he stopped to see what happened to his animal. They took turns firing. One hit the boy's arm, and he looked at it.

Maria cried out so loudly I thought she had been hit. Fear for the boy hit me square in the gut, but there was nothing I could do.

The General intervened. "Mister, take that trashcan and help Ms. Gonzales out to the hall."

Mark did as he was told. Maria wailed until the exit

door slammed, cutting her off. Then Mark was back, but the General had taken his spot. I saw two dots in the sky that I recognized as vultures; they were already circling overhead.

Rider One opened up, cutting into the upright figure.

There were twelve guns firing out there, only four were in range. Rider One spewed lead until the kid dropped down among his flock.

They kept firing. Rider One emptied its gun and hopped on another Johnson to start it all over again. It emptied three stations of ammo, and then disappeared. I couldn't see the boy out there in the sea of dead sheep, but I knew where his body was.

Marketing broke the silence. "How much money did we make on that?"

"That would depend on if Rider One was paying with real credit," I said, raising my voice. "Go figure that out somewhere else, Sir, why don't ya?"

It was as still as the O.K. Corral. The breeze had died with the sheep. You could see the heat rising off the barrel, distorting the air and the view of the bloody wool carpet. The logs were capturing it all.

The first buzzard landed.

The corporate kids went after it, but only one Johnson was in range with ammo left. The third rider nailed it, and the bird fell down behind a sheep.

"Private?"

"Yes, Sir?"

"Is our border secure?"

I checked ammo levels. All the guns in range were empty except two. If it wasn't for them, someone could walk right out of Las Cruce there in the distance and untouched into America. There were a few rounds of protection left.

"Yes, Sir. We're still closed for business, Sir. No sign of Rider One."

"Good. I want your report by 08:00 tomorrow morning. I want your recommendations on how to detect these things, and your thoughts on how to keep these wolves out of our hen house. Rose is right; we can't let this get out, and we can't let it happen again."

"Yes, Sir."

"Rose, we have a Situation Cleansing Directive to attend to before any of this breaks. I'll see you and your staff in my office in ten minutes. And figure out if we have to pay for those sheep."

"Yes, General," she said.

They left me alone with Marketing. He slipped around my chair and pointed at the screen. I cleared my throat and he snatched his hand back.

"Do you think you could--" Marketing said.

"Do you think maybe you could vacate my work station?" I knew what he wanted, and I needed the count for my report anyway, so I launched the image analyzers.

One cactus stump; 69 mesquite bushes; 437 dead sheep.

"Where's the kid?" Marketing asked.

"Probably an error. I'll rerun it."

"No, look there." He pointed but did not touch.

I switched back to the main camera and zoomed in on where the boy had dropped. Something was moving. A hand reached over a dead sheep and clutched wool.

But it wasn't exactly a hand, more like a prosthetic.

A disfigured head followed, dented stainless steel where the boy's fleshy covering had been shot away on the right side. No blood at all. It heaved itself upright, the torso covered in the lace-like remains of a shirt. Sunlight reflected off the thing's chest.

The Johnson within range started shooting.

"This rider better get lucky," I said. "His Johnson only has eleven rounds left."

Another buzzard landed and distracted the rider. I zoomed in as close as I could get to the shepherd. It was clearly a robot of some sort. Probably a Sony someone had adapted for herding near the border Johnsons. It had to be controlled, probably from the Cruce clock tower visible just above that dust cloud.

"I'm no economist," Mark said, "but those robots gotta cost some money, at least two million a pop, right? Whoever is behind that has some serious corporate backing. That's way too much overhead for a couple of sheep. At least nobody died. The General will be happy."

"Yeah," I said, as the buzzard flew apart.

"Nice shot," he said, like he was watching some video game.

I wanted to hit him, but I had to make sure Rider One hadn't come back. It was an engineer, Barry Cutler, recently laid off from a Honda plant in Tennessee. He spent his last two shots, one after the other, into a dead carcass.

There were five rounds left, and Rider One was back onboard.

A buzzard landed. Then another. They walk-hopped from the back of one sheep to another, pecking the eyes out and swallowing them. Two more buzzards glided in, then skittered sideways as a sheep heaved itself up from the hot sand and stumbled off.

I flipped to the rider cam and saw Rider One's crosshairs land on a little red light on the robot's neck. Then it panned away, locking on Johnson after Johnson as if to challenge.

I took control of the only other loaded gun in the corridor. In seconds, Rider One focused on me. Interesting.

"Shoot it," Marketing urged. "You've got four more bullets then it does."

I lowered the barrel, keeping Rider One in view, and shot into the dirt, four times. As expected, Rider One aimed away and buried one likewise.

"What are you doing?"

"Shut up, Sir."

"No, look there."

In another window, I saw the dust cloud was full of vehicles, coming at us fast.

"Get out of my work area, Sir, or I'll call the MPs."

Mark hesitated.

"Leave. Go now." I poked him hard, so there was no mistaking my intent. He backed out, glancing my way until he slipped through the exit.

In the desert, I buried another round. Rider One followed suit. We traded like that two more times until we had one round each. Rider One shot the dirt, nodded his barrel, then pointed it straight up like a flagpole.

My last round kicked up a puff of dust, and I pointed my gun and the other empty units at the sky, praying I was doing the right thing.

Alerts lit up all over my main control screen. My

headset squawked so loud I thought everyone could hear, and I covered the earpiece with a guilty hand.

"We've got a possible open border alert in your sector, Private. Can you confirm?"

I glanced around in case Mark had come back, then saw the caravan stop to clear its path of dead sheep. There were dozens of old trucks with men, women, and children of all ages huddled together inside. More were charging in from Las Cruce now hidden in the distance behind the growing dust cloud.

My heart pounded in my chest. What the hell was I doing?

"Private! Can you confirm?"

Shit. "Sir!" I said, my voice cracking, so I cleared my throat to get it under control and lied. "This should be a low ammo alert, Sir, but there appears to be a malfunction. We're still secure. I'm tracking the problem down now." I took a steadying breath and went on, calmer now. "We had a little action today, so I'll need a priority reload tomorrow, or in the next couple days at the latest."

The first truck passed my gunbot, faces pressed against the dusty windows. Something warm welled up inside me.

"Very well, Private. I'll bump your reload up the list. Carry on." He clicked off.

I leaned back and watched the rider queues stack up on the gunbots out of range as the trucks threaded through. I might have sighed.

"Hey," Dobie called out from next door. "You okay in there?"

I was shaking. Rider One hadn't killed anyone. It had just helped clear the way through. There were bound to be related malfunctions, right?

"Hey? Are you still there?"

I thought I heard Dobie's chair creak like he was getting up, so I turned the gun away from the caravan.

"I'm okay, Dobie. It's just hard to look at empty desert after so much excitement."

That satisfied him. Dobie stayed put and I went back to looking. Unless someone walked in or Marketing squealed on me, I had until the end of my shift to sort this out. I was screwed, yeah, but as I sat watching them come across the border I felt like I could do anything.

"Welcome to America," I whispered.

Thanks for reading!

This short story was first published in 2008 in a special issue of the British Science Fiction Magazine INTERZONE (issue 216) guest edited by Geoff Ryman.

Recent events have made me interested in getting REMOTE CONTROL back out in the world again. I recorded the podcast and sent it along to Interzone Magazine for their podcast site, TRANSMISSIONS FROM BEYOND. TFB is still going, but the podcast of the story was taken down a few years ago. After all, the story was published in June of 2008. Oddly enough, it still reads fresh to me. If you would like to listen to the original TFB Podcast of REMOTE CONTROL hit my website and check the blogs for "My First Podcast."

THIS STORY COULD HAPPEN....

Don't kid yourself. I once explained this story to an acting Marine Colonel at a cocktail party in 2010, a few years after it had been published, and he said, "That's actually a good idea." He turned and walked away leaving me a bit nervous.

This story is about border and immigration control along the Mexican border. It's also about gun rights. It's about how all that can go really, really wrong and how we need to keep believing that good will surface in even the most unlikely places.

R R Angell is a queer writer (pronouns he/him), a graduate of the Clarion West Writers Workshop and a Virginia Center for the Creative Arts fellow. He received a grant from the Maryland State Arts Council in 1999, a Governor's Citation for artistic excellence from the State of Maryland, won the Dana Award for Speculative Fiction in 2000, and the Jenny McKean Writer's Award in Washington, DC in 1996. His work has appeared in Interzone, Asimov's Science Fiction, Gargoyle, The Baltimore Review, among others, and many anthologies including "Sex & Chocolate," "Best Date Ever: True Stories That Celebrate Gay Relationships," and "Stress City."

His work has been translated into French and Chinese.

More at rrangell.com

Sisu Publications

Books against the odds!

Sisu is a Finnish concept that embodies tenacity of purpose, bravery, resilience, hardiness, and resoluteness in the face of adversity. That is why we focus on LGBTQ authors. A short story (this one) and a novelette will publish in 2018. Our first novel offering is in the works. look for it in early 2019.

More at SisuPublications.com

32633018R00019

Made in the USA
Columbia, SC
08 November 2018